MW00575235

Fairy Slippers

Cara Peckham

**For those who dare to dream,
and those who believe in magic,
there is a special gift bestowed.
All you have to do is quiet your mind
and listen carefully,
I bet you will hear them…**

*For Sophia and Ricky ~ my beautiful free spirits, dream big
dreams; mommy will always believe in you.*

*For Mom ~ you dared me to dream, and showed me
the magic. Thank you for always believing.*

In the pale moonlight, when all of the children are asleep, a quiet, hollow drumming can be heard far beyond the cities, towns and villages. Soon the drumming turns into music made up of woodwind and string instruments. Then the jubilant merriment begins; dancing, singing and frolicking commence, for this is the gathering of the fairies. Most humans never hear this celebration. However, a lucky few exist who can quiet their minds just long enough to make out the chatter, laughter and, sometimes, even the music. Some may even be lucky enough to catch a glimpse, although it is rare. Molly was one of the lucky ones, for, as a child, she was lucky enough to have caught a glimpse of the fairy gathering. This is her story…

Molly grew up in a small, New England town, two-miles outside of the city. Her yard was nature's playground. Beautiful gardens bloomed with colorful sprays of wildflowers and a vegetable garden that she and her family tended to all summer. Molly's vegetable garden was filled with the crispiest red leaf lettuce, greenest green peppers and sweetest sweet peas; cucumbers perfect for pickling, and the roundest red beets. Molly, you see, was a kind lover of nature, and just like the fairies, she loved to take care of all living things. The fairies felt safe with Molly, which is precisely why their celebrations took place in her backyard.

Molly loved her yard. She especially loved that there were so many places to
hide. One of her favorite hiding places was deep in the back, where a babbling
brook broke through the trees and was covered by a handmade bridge. Molly
would often cross the bridge to play in the clearing at the edge of the forest.
Little did she know that the bridge was a special hiding place for the delicate
little fairies. They would sometimes leave their instruments behind after
gathering during the night to sing and dance. However, Molly never noticed the
instruments that were left behind.

Molly was always too busy playing to notice that she had something special growing on either side of her handmade bridge, alongside her family's vegetable garden and in the lush wild flower gardens. She didn't even notice that she had this special something growing right outside her bedroom window. What was this special something growing in Molly's yard, that attracted the smallest and most delicate of creatures? It was a little something called jewelweed.

Jewelweed is a weed, but not just any ordinary weed. It's a flowering weed usually found near poison ivy. When placed in water, the leaves sparkle like glittering jewels.

Molly's yard was filled with jewelweed and, yes, a bit of poison ivy, too, which is why the fairies made her yard their home. Fairies know that humans avoid touching poison ivy because touching it can cover them in an itchy rash. Therefore, the fairies felt safe in Molly's yard, snuggled inside the bright orange flower of the jewelweed, guarded by poison ivy.

It wasn't until Molly's seventh birthday that something amazing happened. She began to notice certain things that she hadn't noticed before, like the fact that the moon seemed to follow her no matter where she went at night, or that the clouds took on certain shapes and moved across the sky. She even began to hear sounds she had never stopped to listen to before, like the sweet sounds of the birds chirping their early morning melodies. Molly was becoming more aware of her surroundings. She also became very curious and would often stay up late to listen carefully to the sounds of the night as she looked out her bedroom window. One night, as Molly lay awake, she noticed something she had never seen before. It was a small dot of light bouncing around her ceiling, just above her bedroom window. She hopped out of bed and slowly and cautiously began to walk toward the bouncing light. As she got closer, the light got brighter and brighter. Soon, it was not one bouncing light, but two and then three and, before she knew it, the lights were everywhere, bouncing around her room. Molly decided to climb up onto her toy box and take a look outside. When she did, she couldn't believe her eyes as she saw thousands of bouncing lights. She knew that, without a doubt, she had to go outside and investigate. Molly tiptoed quietly to her closet. She stepped into her quietest shoes, threw her favorite hooded sweatshirt on over her lavender nightgown and made her way outside.

Once outside, Molly got down on her belly and slithered like a snake toward the spot beneath her window. As she edged closer, she saw them, flitting between the jewelweed flowers. They were tiny creatures no bigger than dragonflies. They were singing and flying about, each carrying a single dewdrop.

The fairies flew together as if in a dance. They flew around the yard, carefully placing the dewdrops on the lush flowers, vegetables, and blades of grass.

This process went on for hours until the sun began to appear over the horizon. Then, one-by-one, as Molly watched, each fairy nestled itself inside the tiny jewelweed flower. Molly rushed to get back inside. She didn't want her parents to know that she'd been awake all night. She took off her quiet shoes and her hooded sweatshirt and hopped back into bed. Within a few minutes, she was sound asleep.

Later that morning, Molly made her way to the kitchen where she helped her mom make breakfast. Together, they squeezed the oranges to make orange juice, mixed the batter for pancakes and warmed the maple syrup as the teakettle whistled on the stove.

"Mom," Molly asked quietly, "do you believe in fairies?"

"I sure do," her mom said. "Why?"

"Well," Molly began, "can I show you something after breakfast?"

"Of course," her mom said. "We'll eat and then you can show me. How does that sound?"

"Great!" Molly exclaimed.

After breakfast, Molly led the way outside.

"Where are we going?" her mom asked.

"Don't worry, mom. You're going to love what you're about to see," Molly said, grinning from ear to ear.

When they reached the spot under Molly's bedroom window, Molly sat down. Her mother knelt beside her.

"What are we looking at, Molly?"

"The flowers," Molly said.

"Oh dear, these are not flowers; these are weeds. They are not just any ordinary weeds though," her mom said. "This right here, is called jewelweed."

"Jewelweed?" Molly repeated.

"Yes," her mom said, "jewelweed. This pretty little flower is actually very useful. It can be used as a remedy for poison ivy."

"Poison ivy?" Molly asked.

"Yes, although I don't see any right here, it is all around and you must be careful. You wouldn't want to get poison ivy."

"Why not?" Asked Molly.

"Poison ivy can cause an itchy rash," her mom explained.

"An itchy rash?" Molly asked, as she scratched her arm.

"Yes, an itchy rash." Her mom giggled. "When I was a little girl, I too, heard the music and saw the fairies dancing into the wee hours of the night."

"You did?" Molly asked in amazement

"I certainly did," her mom replied.

"It is called the gathering of the fairies. That is what my mother, your grandmother, used to call it. She had a special name for these tiny, orange flowers. Would you like to know what she called them?"

"Yes, yes, of course!" Molly said excitedly as she edged her way closer to her mother.

"FAIRY SLIPPERS!" her mom exclaimed. "Grandma used to say that fairies do not want to be seen or heard by humans. Instead, they prefer to go about their business, handling all of their jobs in nature, quietly. She said that if fairies were spotted by humans, not all, but most humans, might want to capture them, put them in jars and leave them helpless, unable to take care of and preserve our Earth. This is why fairies are very clever in choosing where they make their homes. You know, Molly, it is a special gift to be able to see and hear them."

"I'm lucky, aren't I mom?" Molly asked.

"Yes, Molly, you are very lucky," her mom said, nodding.

"Can you still see them Mom? Can you still see the fairies?'

"No, Molly. Sadly, I haven't been able to see or hear them for quite some time, but I can remember how wonderful it was." Her mom smiled and held Molly tight.

Later that night, after Molly went to bed, she was suddenly awakened by a sound. She sat up in her bed and listened carefully. Could it be? Could it be the fairy gathering? She thought for a moment and then raced to the window. Sadly, she saw nothing. However, she could hear the faint sound of hollow drumming mixed with the sounds of woodwind and string instruments playing. The sounds seemed to be getting louder. At the other end of the hall, her mom lay awake. She, too, could hear the sounds getting louder and louder. Could it be? Could it be the fairy gathering? Molly's mom hopped out of bed and raced to Molly's bedroom. As quick as she could, she swung open the door.

There, in front of the window, she saw Molly staring out into the moonlit sky. Molly's mom joined her at the window and, together, they waited and watched.

All of a sudden, they saw the most beautiful sight. One-by-one, the fairies flew out of the fairy slippers and began their work spreading the dewdrops on all of the lush flowers, vegetables and blades of grass.

As they stood there and watched, Molly looked at her mom and said in a whisper,

"Isn't is spectacular, Mommy?"

"Yes, yes, dear, it is."

Molly's mom held Molly in her arms and the two watched in amazement, until the sun peered over the horizon.

What Molly didn't realize that night, as she stood next to her mother in front of the window, was that the fairies had more in store for her. Molly's adventures were not over, in fact, they were just beginning…

CPSIA information can be obtained
at www.ICGtesting.com
Printed in the USA
BVHW021204230821
615023BV00005B/96